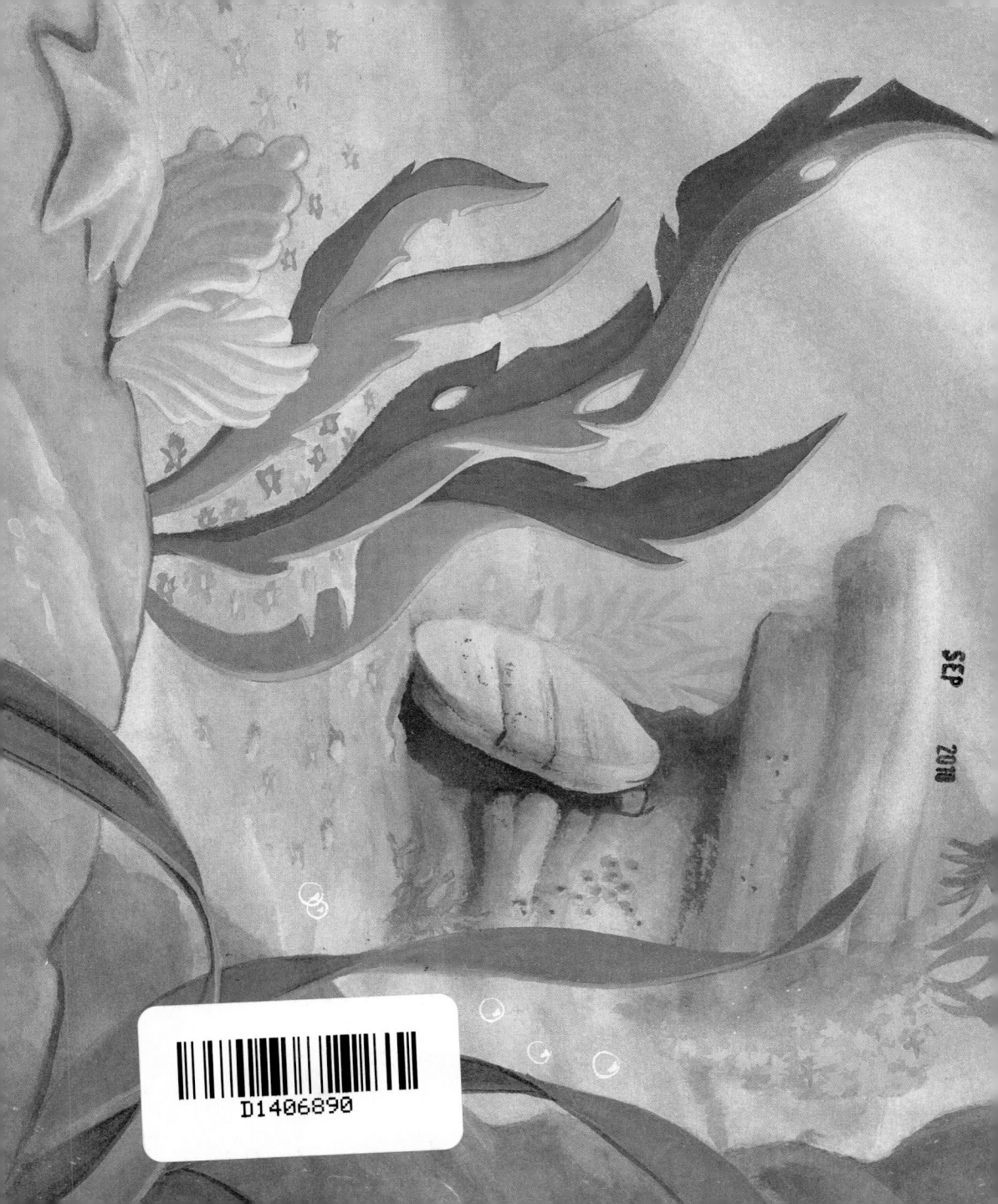

Grolier Books

Produced by Kroha Associates, Inc.
Middletown, Connecticut

Illustrated by Yakovetic Productions

Printed in the United States of America.

ISBN 0-7172-8397-6

An Undersea Wish

Once every ten years, a very, very rare sea flower called the flaminia blooms for one day — and one day only. Legend has it that whoever sees the beautiful blossom first will be granted any wish his heart desires — but only if he is the only one watching when the flower opens its petals.

Flounder the fish had been waiting secretly for that special day to arrive. He had marked it on his calendar, and now it was here. Flounder was sure he was the only one who had remembered the legend, and he couldn't wait to make his wish.

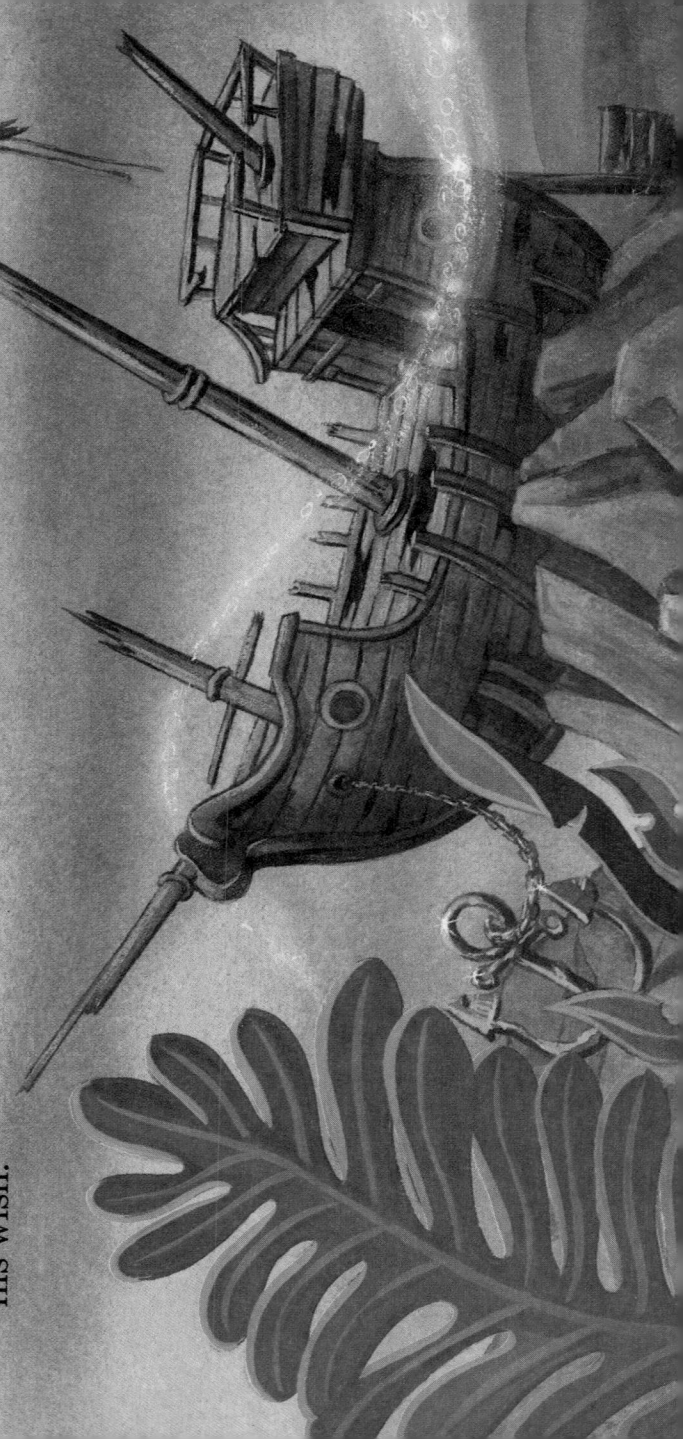

As the first faint rays of morning light slowly crept across the ocean floor on that special day, Flounder was already on his way to keep watch over the flaminia.

When he reached the place where the flower grew, he nestled in a nearby patch of seaweed and practiced making his wish. "I want to be famous, and important, and loved," he whispered over and over again.

Flounder *thought* he was the only one who had remembered the legend, but the evil sea witch, Ursula, had remembered it, too. And she had a wish of her own.

"Today's the day I become the ruler of the seas," Ursula said to her eels, Flotsam and Jetsam, as she peered greedily into her magic pearl. The pearl let Ursula see what was going on anywhere under the ocean. "I've waited ten years and now — wait! What's this? That horrible little fish Flounder is watching over *my* flower! He'll ruin everything! I must get rid of him so *my* wish will be the one that comes true!"

"Flotsam! Jetsam!" Ursula cried when she had thought of a plan. "Go and tell Flounder that you heard the Little Mermaid yelling for help. That will get rid of him for sure, and then the magic power of the flaminia will be all mine!"

"Ariel in trouble? I've got to help her!" Flounder said when the eels had delivered their message. *If I leave now,* he thought to himself, *the flaminia might bloom while I'm gone, and then I won't be able to make my wish.* But deep down Flounder knew it was more important to help his friend. He put aside his selfish thoughts and raced off.

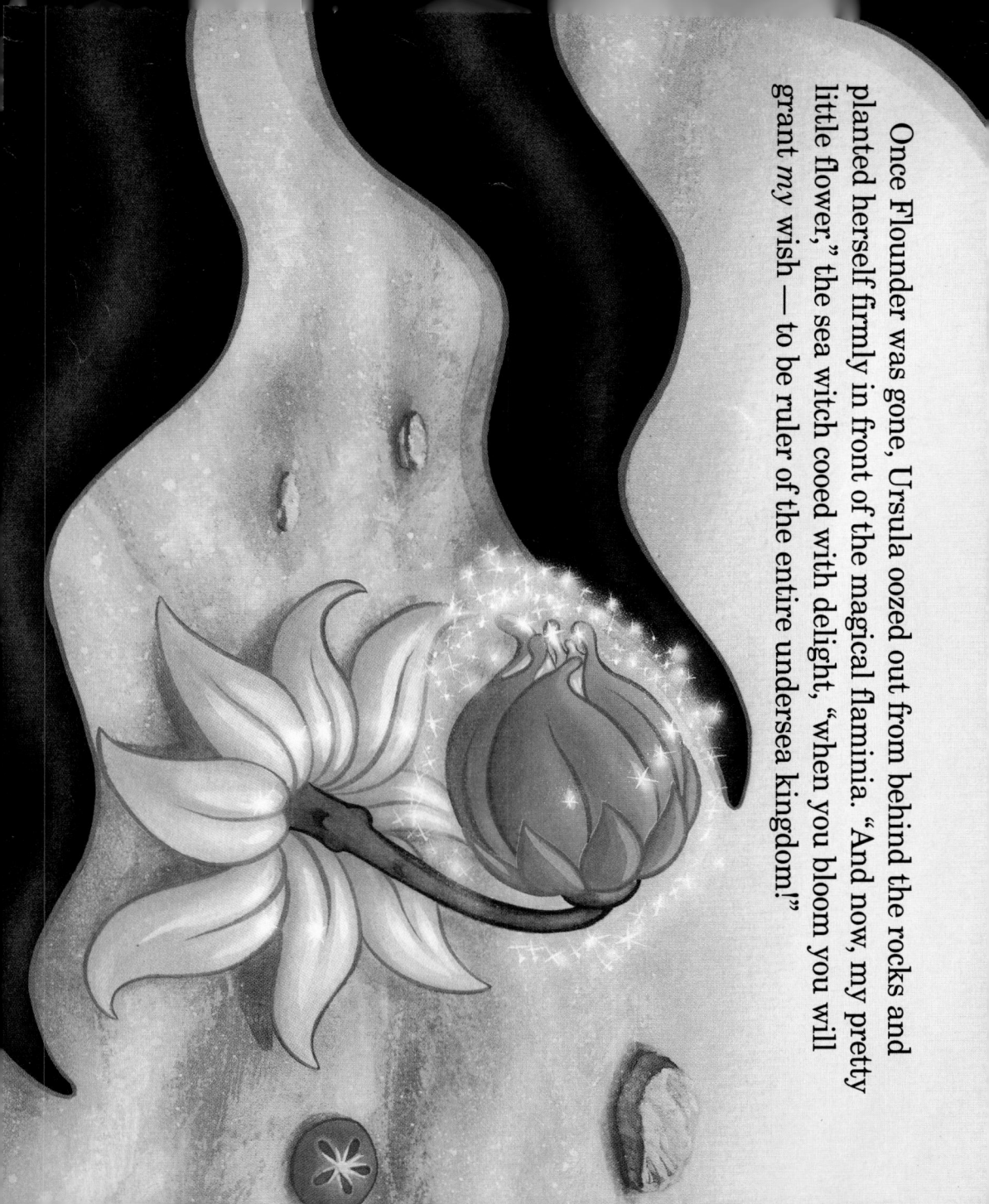

Once Flounder was gone, Ursula oozed out from behind the rocks and planted herself firmly in front of the magical flaminia. "And now, my pretty little flower," the sea witch cooed with delight, "when you bloom you will grant *my* wish — to be ruler of the entire undersea kingdom!"

Flounder was exhausted by the time he reached Ariel. "I came just as soon as I heard you needed help," he said when he had caught his breath. "What's wrong?"

"Why, nothing's wrong," replied the Little Mermaid. "In fact, Sandy and Sebastian and I were just going to play a game of hide-and-seek. Would you like to join us?"

"The eels tricked me!" Flounder pouted. "Now I'll never get my wish!"

"What are you talking about?" asked Sandy.

"The magic flower!" Flounder replied. "Today is the day it's supposed to bloom, and if I'm the only one who sees it, then my wish will come true."

Then Flounder told them how he remembered the legend of the flower, and how excited he was about making his wish. "But it's probably too late now. Ursula must be there already," he said sadly.

"Why, I had forgotten all about that silly old legend," Sebastian laughed. "You don't really believe the flaminia is magical, do you, Flounder? How could there be such a thing as a wish-granting flower?"

But Flounder refused to listen. "It's true," he said stubbornly. "I just know it's true."

The Little Mermaid hated to see her friend looking so sad. "Maybe it's not too late," she told him. "If you hurry, you might still be the first to see the flaminia bloom, and make your wish."

"Maybe you're right!" Flounder said, swimming away as fast as his little tail would move him. He was in such a hurry, that he nearly ran into King Triton.

"Where is Flounder rushing off to?" the king asked.

"Oh, he's got some silly notion in his head about a magical flower that will grant him one wish," replied Sebastian with a chuckle.

"The legend of the flaminia," said King Triton. "I'd almost forgotten! You know, Sebastian, since no one has ever seen the blooming alone, we really don't know — that legend might just be true."

Ariel told her father the rest of the story, about how Ursula had tricked Flounder into leaving before the flower bloomed. "This is terrible!" cried the king. "We must hurry and get there before the blooming! If Ursula is the only one there when the flower opens, you can be sure she'll make a wish that will harm us all!"

But Ursula *was* the only one there, and as the petals of the beautiful flower started to unfold, she began to make her wish....

"My wish," hissed the sea witch, "is to be the ruler of everything under the —"

But before she could finish, Flounder came swooshing up. He was in such a hurry that he didn't even see the evil witch. "I see it! I see it!" he cried. "Now I'll get my wish after all!"

"You foolish little fish!" Ursula shouted at Flounder. "You've ruined everything! Now I'll have to wait *ten more years* for what is rightfully mine! I'll teach you to get in *my way!*"

Ursula lunged toward Flounder, but King Triton and the others arrived just in time to stop her. "Leave here at once!" the king demanded. "As the one and only *true* ruler of the sea, I order you to go!"

"I'll go," replied the sea witch, "but I'll be back the next time the flaminia blooms, and then we'll see who is ruler of the sea!"

Later, King Triton declared it Flounder Day, in honor of Flounder's bravery and concern for his friends. The little fish had spoiled Ursula's plans to rule the sea, and all its creatures knew of the wonderful thing he had done. "I'm sorry you weren't able to find out if the legend about the flower was true," Ariel said to her friend. "Now you won't get your wish."

"But my wish *did* come true," Flounder replied. "Flounder Day has made me important *and* famous, and with friends like you, I know I'll always be loved, too."

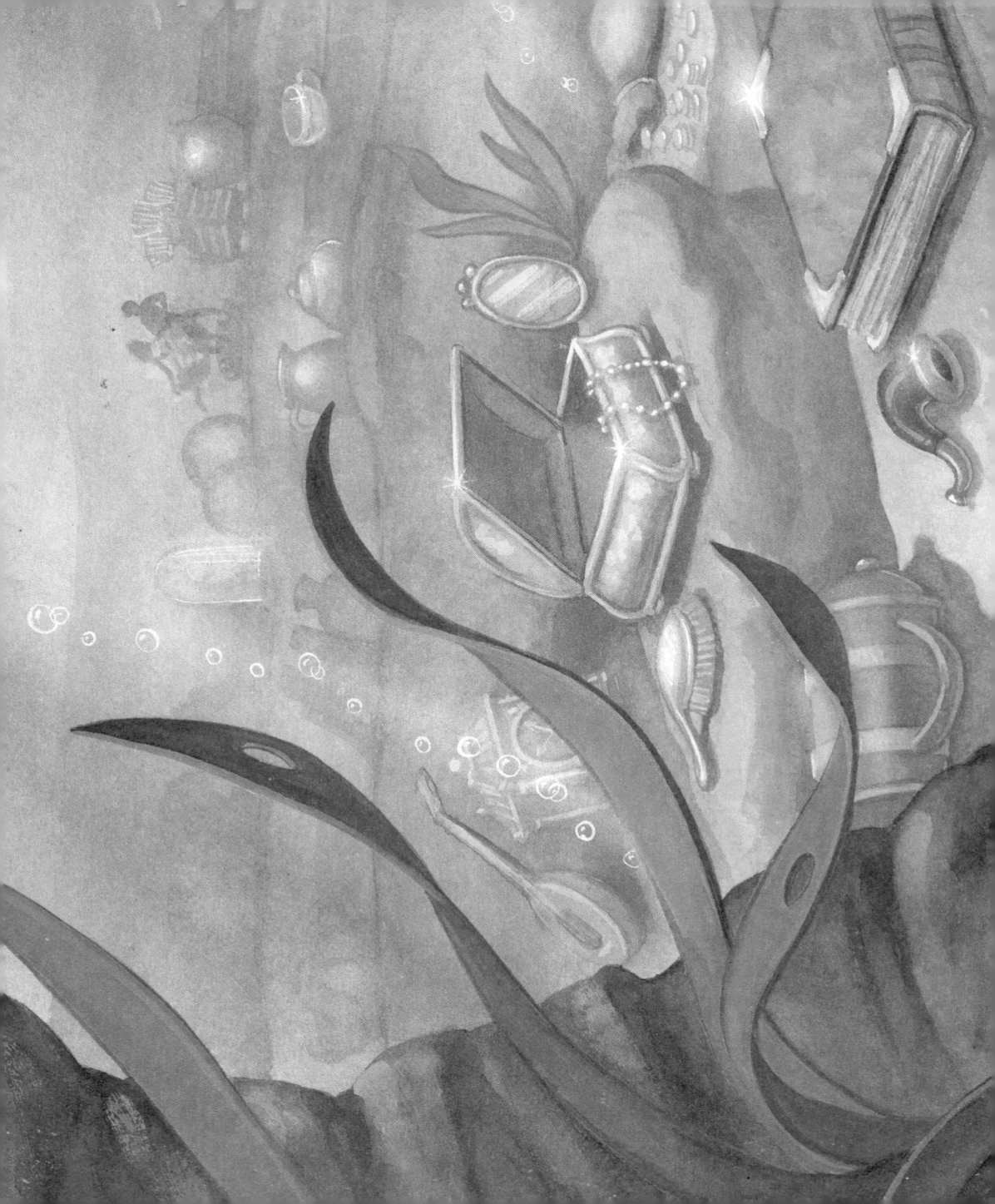